ZACH RILEY
SURPRISE KICK

Text by Tad Kershner
Illustrated by Andrés Martínez Ricci

Published by ABDO Publishing Company, PO Box 398166,
Minneapolis, MN 55439. Copyright © 2013 by Abdo Consulting Group,
Inc. International copyrights reserved in all countries. No part of this
book may be reproduced in any form without written permission
from the publisher. SportsZone™ is a trademark and logo of ABDO
Publishing Company.

Printed in the United States of America,
North Mankato, Minnesota
052012
092012

Text by: Tad Kershner
Illustrator: Andrés Martínez Ricci

Editor: Chrös McDougall
Series Designer: Craig Hinton

Library of Congress Cataloging-in-Publication Data
Riley, Zach.
  Surprise kick / by Zach Riley ; illustrated by Andres Ricci ; text by Tad
Kershner.
     p. cm. -- (Zach Riley)
  Summary: Fifth-grader Cody Ross considers himself a champion
at soccer--video-game soccer, that is--but now that his parents have
taken away his toys and insisted that he join a team he is finding out
that he has a lot to learn about soccer, teamwork and friendship.
  ISBN 978-1-61783-536-0
  1. Soccer stories. 2. Teamwork (Sports)--Juvenile fiction. 3. Self-
confidence--Juvenile fiction. 4. Friendship--Juvenile fiction. [1. Soccer-
-Fiction. 2. Teamwork (Sports)--Fiction. 3. Self-confidence--Fiction. 4.
Friendship--Fiction.] I. Martinez Ricci, Andres, ill. II. Kershner, Tad,
1967- III. Title.
  PZ7.R4572Sur 2012
  813.6--dc23
                              2012007906

TABLE OF CONTENTS

ONE 4

TWO 11

THREE 22

FOUR 32

FIVE 42

SIX 50

SEVEN 60

EIGHT 66

ONE

Cody Ross sat in his fifth grade math class. Yet all he could think about was the World Cup trophy.

Of course, it wasn't a real trophy. Cody's friend the Mudman had made it up the summer before. The trophy was made of tin foil, and it was supposed to look like a star. There was a dent in one of the points from where Cody's cat Cooper had gnarled it. But Cody still thought it was a pretty cool trophy.

School was when Cody was supposed to be learning. But as Mrs. Stoutner wrote out a long division problem on the whiteboard, his mind kept drifting back to that trophy. Cody could see it in his head. The game is on the line. His team has a free kick. Cody lines up, and then lofts the ball toward a streaking teammate's head.

"Cody."

It was Mrs. Stoutner. She called Cody up to the board to answer one of the math problems. After a moment, the answer came to Cody and he was back at his desk, thinking about soccer.

The day seemed to take forever. The only thing that made it go faster—or maybe it was slower—was thinking about soccer.

Finally, at three o'clock, the bell rang. Cody was halfway down the steps before he realized that he might have forgotten to write down tomorrow's homework.

∭

Cody caught up with Mud just as they got onto the bus. He fished the crumpled piece of notebook paper out of his pocket and showed it to his friend.

"Who's first?" Mud asked.

They looked down at the single-elimination tournament bracket, with none of the eight teams filled out.

"I'll take Germany," Cody answered.

"Fine, I've got Brazil."

They went back and forth, picking four teams each and scribbling their names into the bracket. It was such a fierce discussion for who would get Argentina that they almost missed Cody's bus stop.

"Fine, you can have them!" Cody yelled as they scrambled off the bus. "I'll take Ghana, and I'll whoop you with them!"

But when they burst into Cody's living room, his world fell out from under him.

"Dad! We've been robbed!"

《《《《《

Cody's dad, Richard, was whistling in the kitchen, where it smelled like he was making something with tomatoes and garlic. Probably something he saw on *Cooking Quest.*

Cody thought that his dad wasn't nearly as worried as he should have been. Cody ran into the kitchen and grabbed his dad's hand. It was all sticky from peeling shrimp.

"Eww!" Cody wiped his hand on his jeans and dragged his dad to the living room by his apron.

"Didn't you hear me? We've been robbed!"

Richard patted Cody on the head and got stinky shrimp guts in his hair.

"We haven't been robbed," he said. "I've been here all afternoon."

Cody looked again. His dad was right. The TV was still there. So was the DVD player, the cable box, and Richard's watch, which was sitting on the end table.

What wasn't there, though, was Cody's gaming stuff. Not the console, not the controllers, and especially not the games. It was all gone.

How was he going to play soccer now?

Stunned, Cody ran and checked behind the couch. Still nothing. He looked back at Richard. Why was he smiling?

"Dad? Anything you want to tell me?" Cody said, now sounding a bit worked up. "Where's my gaming stuff?"

"It's taking a little break," Richard said calmly. "Your mom and I had a talk."

Uh oh, thought Cody.

"You're scaring me, Dad. What are you talking about?"

A dangerous spattering sound came from the kitchen, and Richard ran back in like he was chasing down the perfect through pass. When Cody and Mud got there, Richard was stirring two different pots and grinning. Leaving the pots to bubble, Richard reached under the sink and grabbed something. He threw it to Cody.

A soccer ball.

TWO

Cody and Mud both scrambled after the soccer ball, and Cody bowled Mud into the coffee table. Cody picked himself from the jumble and held up the ball. It looked so old it could've belonged to Pelé himself.

Cody's dad was stirring the pot again.

"That's the ball from my championship game in high school," he said.

"You never told me you played in the championship!"

Richard smiled. "Not the school championship. This neighborhood thing we had, me and Stewie Duncan."

"You had a friend named Stewie?"

"Your best friend's name is Mudman."

Mudman looked up at Richard.

"I'm thinking of changing it to 'The Mud,'" he said. "What do you think, Mr. Ross?"

Cody elbowed Mud. "Don't change the subject," he whispered, then called back to his dad, "Where's my stuff?"

"Your mom and I decided it's time you try some real soccer for a change."

"But Dad—"

"You don't think real World Cup players spend all their time inside playing the games out on a gaming system, do you?"

Of course they did, thought Cody. At least they probably did at night.

Cody's dad slurped some of the sauce from his big wooden spoon. "You'll get your stuff back when you've played a whole season."

"Daaad!" Cody protested. "You were always telling me about the bruises and sprained ankles you got when you played!"

His dad just grinned this crazy grin at him. "That's the fun of it, son!"

〽〽〽

Cody had to think quickly. This couldn't really be happening. He loved soccer. In fact, he loved pretty much all sports. But he loved to play them on video games. The real thing? That just wasn't for Cody. He had to do something, and fast! He grabbed Mud.

"Dinner's in 37 minutes," Richard called after them. "Don't be late. It's going to be good."

At first, Cody didn't say a word to Mud. He was thinking. Cody knew there must be some way out of having to join the soccer team. He just needed to find his dad's weak spot.

Cody and Mud found Cody's mom Becky outside, weeding the Thai basil.

Cody put on his best scared look. "Dad wants to ruin me!"

Becky gave him this bright huge mom smile. "We're worried about you just sitting in front of the TV all day. We think you need to get some time in the fresh air, outdoors."

Cody knew he had to fight back. "Fall's coming on. I hear it's going to be raining a lot. Then the snow's going to hit us hard. You don't want your only son out there getting colds and stuff. The flu is supposed to be really bad this year."

"You'll love it. You'll see." She wrenched out one particularly giant weed. "It's just one season."

That was a whole lot of days to be smashed into the mud. Cody preferred his big rocking chair, which rolled all the way so that the back touched the ground, to the cold and the mud.

"But Mom," Cody pleaded. "I could be paralyzed for life. One of those big guys slams into me and BOOM! You're visiting me in the hospital and feeding me dinner through a straw."

Becky stayed cool. Cody had to admire her for that. She ran one muddy glove along his cheek and kissed him on the forehead. "Cody, honey. It was my idea."

Suddenly Cody felt like he was the last defender between Lionel Messi and the goal—utterly helpless.

The next day, Richard took Cody and Mud to sign-ups for the Lincoln Street Lions. Mud didn't have to go, but he hated playing against the computer, so he figured he'd give real soccer a shot too.

The first sight of a Lions practice made Cody and Mud stop in their tracks.

The team was hardcore. The players were all fifth graders, but they looked like they had been playing for years. Some kids did wind sprints and zigzagged between a bunch of cones for agility training. Others were in a juggling group, trying to see how long they could keep the ball off the ground.

"Come on," said Mud. "They look pretty cool."

They looked pretty good. Too good.

Turning and booking it back to the car seemed like a really good choice, but Mud was halfway across the field already. Cody couldn't let him get there first.

Two of the guys introduced themselves as Mahender and Trong.

"The Mud," said Mud.

"I'm Cody," said Cody. "Cody Ross."

"Get ready to win this season!" said Mud. "Codes is amazing! Once he made this incredible free kick where he curved it around—"

Cody elbowed Mud hard and muttered through his teeth so no one else could hear. "What are you doing?"

"They gotta know what a soccer genius they get to play with!"

"Go easy on all that genius stuff! Under-promise and over-deliver, that's what my dad always says."

"It'll be no sweat for you! You've got all the plays in your head. How much different can it be?"

Cody looked up at the group of players who were juggling the ball together, kicking if off their feet, knees, and head with the ease of a video game character.

Pretty different, thought Cody.

Just then, this kid with a face like a ferret came over from the wind sprints and trapped the ball on a dime right next to Cody. He wasn't even breathing hard.

"You tryin' out for striker?" ferret guy asked.

Cody didn't want to get on anyone's bad side already. "Um . . . I dunno. I was thinkin' about maybe—"

"What's wrong with you?" the other boy scowled. "Striker's the only position worth playing. I wouldn't trust a guy who didn't at least dream about bein' striker."

"Sure I am," said Cody. "But you guys have been playing together a lot longer. Probably got your moves all worked out already. I wouldn't want to mess anybody up."

"Let Coach Parks figure that out. You gotta' at least try for it." The boy grinned. "Otherwise you'll be on defense—at my mercy."

Before Cody could say anything, a guy with a beard and twinkling eyes blew a whistle. "Liiiiine Uuuuup!"

It was Coach Parks. He was a pretty laid-back looking guy—the kind of who guy who might be understanding of Cody's dilemma.

But as much as Cody wanted to get off to a good start with Coach Parks, he couldn't move. Right then, he saw the cutest girl he'd ever seen. She had soft brown eyes and long brown hair. She smiled and waved at him as she lined up along with the boys.

Maybe this wasn't going to be so bad after all, Cody thought.

The next thing he knew, something smashed straight into him and knocked him flat on the ground.

When his head cleared, he looked up to see Ferret Face standing over him.

"That's Amanda Mitchell," said the boy. "And she was waving at ME. You don't talk to her, you don't smile at her. You don't even look at her. Got it?"

THREE

Coach Parks blew his whistle again. Cody felt like the whole team was staring at him. He picked himself off the ground and hustled to join Mud on the center line.

"Count off!" the coach called out, signaling it was time for a scrimmage.

Suddenly everyone was taking turns saying "Red! Blue! Red! Blue!"

When it got to Cody, he shouted out "Red!" in his best team-player voice.

Mudman said "Blue!" and it hit Cody like a whole truckload of soccer balls.

They were going to be on different teams.

That couldn't be happening! Cody and Mud had been connected at the hip for as long as they could remember.

"Get your pinnies!" shouted Coach Parks.

Everybody trotted off and picked up a dorky mesh vest from the red pile or the blue pile. They smelled like they hadn't been washed since the last ice age.

As he followed the others, Cody's mind worked like it was solving a long division problem. Maybe he could tell Mud to *accidentally* grab a red vest. But then the teams wouldn't come out even, and he'd be making a scene on his first day.

"Any time, Ross! We wanna get some play in today!"

It was Ryan—Ferret Face. Cody could tell that he was already becoming Ryan's favorite person.

"Mahender, Luis: Captains!" shouted out Coach Parks.

Coach Parks took out a shiny quarter and polished it on his sleeve. Then he flipped it into the air.

Mahender called "Tails!" and won, so Team Red got the kickoff.

Mudman waved a mournful goodbye as he trotted over to join Ryan on Team Blue.

Cody thought that Mud looked very alone all the way over there. He decided to go easy on him. After all, Mud wasn't the greatest soccer mind—at least when it came to video games. Cody couldn't figure out why Mud still liked to play even when he lost so much.

Coach Parks blew his whistle. Mahender kicked the ball far into the Blue end of the field. Cody and the rest of the Red players surged forward. Ryan got the ball and ran with it, dribbling forward while the Blue defenders closed in on him.

Cody marked Mud, sticking close to his friend on the other side of the field. As a new player, Mud probably wouldn't get much action, so he was the safest place to hide out. Besides, Cody wanted to help his friend in case the team ever charged him.

Ryan passed the ball sideways to Amanda, who was instantly swarmed. Maybe all the Red guys liked her as much as Cody did.

Cody had wondered why Amanda wanted to play on the boys' team. He quickly found out. She eluded one defender by effortlessly rolling the ball underneath her and turning the other way. Then she stood strong and held her back into another defender, keeping him away from the ball.

But pretty soon, it became clear there was no way out. So she passed the ball forward.

To Mud!

Now the entire Red team ran at Mud. Cody felt bad for him. He'd have his pocket picked on the first touch of his first real game.

The defenders would swarm him. If Mud was lucky, he might avoid being knocked to the ground.

Cody nearly closed his eyes, but he had to watch the oncoming train wreck.

Somehow Mud danced clear of them all.

He squeezed between Mitch and Hans, then broke free of the pack, dodging and weaving down the field.

Cody wondered when Mud had gotten so fast.

Mahender ran at Mud full speed. Mud spun away, twisting out of range just as Mahender kicked for the ball.

Then Mitch came in for a sideways snag, but Mud lined up and kicked the ball as hard as he could.

The ball flew into the net above the goalie's head for the first goal of the game.

Cody had never seen a play like that, not even on *Soccer Slam*.

The whole Blue team gathered around Mud, hugging and high-fiving him.

Although Cody tried as hard as he could for the next 19 gajillion hours, he got no closer to the ball than if it had been in another state.

Finally, on the last play of the day, with his belly empty and his whole body feeling like angry rhinoceroses had trampled it, Cody watched the ball actually soaring through the air toward him.

Finally, he had his chance to show everybody on his new team how awesome he was!

Cody tried trapping the ball with his chest, but he quickly found himself sprinting after it when it rolled away from him.

He felt like he was on fire as he rocketed for the goal line.

Maybe his dad was right. Maybe this was better than the console.

Maybe he'd get a real World Cup trophy someday!

Cody lined up for the shot. He planted his left leg. He pulled back his right leg.

WHIFF!

Suddenly the ball was missing—all Cody got was air.

Cody lost his balance and wound up on his backside. One thought ran through his mind as he sat in the grass, watching the play resume back down toward the other end of the field.

The person who had stolen the ball—and made Cody look silly—was the same "loyal till I die" pal who'd been Cody's video game punching bag since third grade.

Cody's backstabbing best friend was Homer "Mud" Modillius.

FOUR

Cody couldn't believe it. The same Mudman who has lost countless games of *Soccer Slam* in Cody's living room had stripped the ball from Cody like it was nothing more than pressing the B button and holding down the X button for a speed burst.

To make matters worse, after rushing down the field Mud had made a perfect pass to Amanda, who placed it right into the back corner of the net.

Cody didn't do much for the rest of practice. How could he? He was stunned.

Mud came over once to ask if Cody was having fun. But Cody just ignored Mud and yelled that he was open—even though he wanted nothing to do with the soccer ball.

Finally, after what felt like a thousand hours, Richard arrived to pick up the boys.

Mud took one look at the scowl on Cody's face and offered to walk.

Richard shook his head. "I promised your parents I'd drive you."

Mud piled in.

"Bet that wasn't so bad, was it?" asked Dad.

Mud jerked forward, ready to explode with news about how much fun he'd had. But then he looked over and saw Cody slouched in his seat. He was clearly in no mood to talk.

"It was fine, Mr. Ross," Mud said plainly.

When they dropped Mud off, the Rosses were about to drive away when Mud stuck his head back in the window.

"Sorry if I embarrassed you on that play, Codes."

Cody didn't look at him. "No biggie," he said. "That's what you do in soccer."

In his heart Cody knew that was true. Mud was on the other team. He was supposed to try to steal the ball from Cody. But that didn't make it any easier.

"What was that about?" Richard asked as they drove away.

"I'm the worst player on the team!"

Dad looked at Cody. "I know it can be hard at first—"

Cody couldn't stop the words pouring out. "I don't care if I never get my games back. Just don't make me go out there again!"

"I know you don't mean that."

Cody had never meant anything more in his whole life. Dad pulled the car into the driveway. Cody wanted to bolt through the door, but Richard reached over and held it.

"Just give it your best shot. No one cares if you win or lose. You just have to play the best you can and have fun."

Had parents never even been kids? Cody wondered. Where do they get stuff like that?

"It was only your first practice. You're playing against kids that have been playing for a long time. You'll get better."

"I'll never get better. Not in a million, billion, trillion years."

///////

And Cody was right. He didn't get better. At least not by much.

After each practice, Cody kept expecting his dad to show just the littlest, tiniest sliver of mercy. But Richard was always endlessly cheerful when he dropped Cody and Mud off and endlessly cheerful when he picked them up.

Richard worked with Cody in the backyard. They passed together, and Cody worked on his dribbling. Cody felt pretty good in the backyard, but as soon as he got back to practice it was as if he had never touched a soccer ball in his life.

He thought Richard might finally let up when he stayed to watch one of the Lions' practices. But afterward Richard just tousled Cody's hair and called out the one play that he hadn't actually biffed and said, "Great job!"

How does he do that? Cody wondered.

Cody still wasn't sure how he felt about Mud. In a way, he was happy to see Mud do so well. But something about Mud's success made Cody feel jealous. Deep down, Cody wanted to be even better than Mud.

Two weeks into practice, he finally saw his chance. He was nearly alone in the goal box when Mahender kicked a long pass to him.

The second Cody saw the ball come soaring through the air at him, he knew this was going to be a thing of beauty, a play for the history books. Cody Ross would be remembered for this play all season!

Zachary Murfin, the Blue goalie, was clear on the other side of the goal. All Cody had to do was jump at just the right time, at just the right angle, and he'd be able to head the ball right into the old onion bag!

Cody saw it all in his mind.

Then he jumped . . . but instead of hitting the ball right on the top of his head, he caught it full in the face.

The ball crunched into his nose and flew sideways.

Cody's whole face stung where the ball had slammed into it, and his eyes teared up.

Landing, he lost his footing on the slick grass and went down in a heap, blood running from his nose.

Fighting back the tears, Cody only dimly heard the coach blow his whistle.

He tried to protest and keep everyone from making a big fuss over him, but his nose would not stop bleeding, and it felt like his eye was starting to swell up.

This was *not* how he wanted to be remembered.

FIVE

In just a couple of weeks Cody had lost his console, his best friend, and now his self-respect.

Nice going, Dad, Cody thought.

He wondered how it could possibly get worse. Then came the day he'd been dreading even more than that disaster called practice. It was time for the season-opener against the Watertown Waves.

First thing when Cody got up, he gave his dad his best sick cough—kind of hoarse and kind of mucousy. He'd been practicing all week, so he thought it was pretty good.

Richard just pointed his finger at Cody and said: "Don't even."

The Waves were about the biggest guys Cody had ever seen. He figured they were either mostly eighth graders or they'd been seriously held back. Cody could swear one of them was even growing a mustache, although it might have just been a pudding stain. And those black clouds in the sky didn't look that great either.

The Waves won the coin toss and decided to take the opening kickoff. For the first time, Cody and Mud were on the same team. So were Ryan and Amanda and Mahender and Trong and everybody else. Ryan was lined up at striker. But it was Mud, not Cody, who lined up next to him. Cody was off to the side as the right midfielder.

The ref blew his whistle and the Waves opened play. Cody's stomach felt like he'd just swallowed a whole string of firecrackers.

The game was barely two minutes old when Cody found himself on his back looking painfully up at the kid with the "mustache."

The ref blew his whistle and held up a yellow card. "This is soccer, not rugby," the ref said. "We kick the ball, not the other players!"

The Watertown kid held out his hand. But when Cody reached for it, the kid yanked it away and ran it through his hair. He laughed his head off like he was the first person ever to think of that joke.

The joke was on him, though. He had knocked Cody over in the penalty area. That meant the Lions got a penalty kick. Coach Parks called for Cody to take it. Cody acted like he was going to go to the left, but then at the last minute twisted his foot to hook the ball to the right.

It was a pretty good kick, but the Waves' goalie knocked it out.

Ryan got the ball off the throw-in. He passed sideways to Amanda, who dribbled five yards and kicked a long air pass to Trong. By that time, Cody had broken away and he was wide open, running as fast as he could. Apparently the Waves didn't think Cody was worth covering. Cody knew that Trong saw him. But Trong tried to run instead of passing and a big Waves player stole the ball.

As the game wore on, the Waves scored three times. Cody felt pretty useless with no one covering him and no one passing to him.

Maybe he'd be better at playing defense.

The second half had just started when the Waves intercepted a pass and quickly began mounting an attack. The Lions' players were too far away to mount a defense. Except Cody.

Cody ran hard for the penalty area. He knew right where the other player was running and raced to beat the player to the spot.

Cody and the other player met just outside the goalie box, but the other kid pulled the ball back just as Cody got there. Cody tried to stop himself but instead fell to the ground. When he turned around, he saw the Waves player pass the ball to a teammate on the other side of the goal.

Cody stretched his leg out. He managed to hit the ball with the tip of his right foot.

Unfortunately for Cody, he hit the ball straight into his own goal.

He'd managed to score for the Waves.

Cody hung his head in shame. Could he not do *anything* right?

As if that wasn't bad enough, the sky opened up and started dumping sheets of cold rain. As Cody shivered with goose bumps growing up his arms, he couldn't help but think how little it rained in his living room.

Then it really started raining, turning the whole field into a slippery, gooey pudding. It was nearly impossible to change direction without sliding, and forget about stopping! The longer they played, the more they got covered in mud.

Soon it was impossible to tell who was whom by their jerseys, which were all now uniformly brown. The rest of the game seemed to last about a thousand years. When the referee finally blew his whistle, the Waves had won 5–0.

Cody was soaked and near freezing to death. His feet ached and squelched in his squishy socks every time he took a step. Cody hated squishy socks.

The rest of his clothes were about 2 percent clothes and 98 percent mud.

His teeth were chattering so fast he could cut boards with them, and he was shivering so violently that he thought he'd rattle apart at any moment.

As Richard pulled up, Cody was all ready for more of his "you-can-do-it" optimism.

Is Dad ever going to be surprised, thought Cody.

He squished into the car, getting up the nerve to say goodbye to his gaming stuff forever. He was quitting the team.

SIX

"Hey Codes," Richard said. "How'd you like to visit grandpa tomorrow?"

Nothing about soccer?

Cody loved going to Grandpa Roy's, because he told the best stories. Suddenly Cody wasn't so cold or wet anymore.

They spent most of Saturday at the Flight Museum. Grandpa Roy knew Cody loved airplanes. And, of course, Grandpa had been a pilot during the Vietnam War. Grandpa once declared he could fly anything that flew, except maybe dragonflies.

After dinner, Grandpa Roy dished out two giant bowls of homemade strawberry ice cream.

He always saved his best stories for Saturday night ice cream time.

"One minute I was swooping in low over the quiet jungle, and the next, it erupted in gunfire," Grandpa recalled, guiding his spoon through the air as if it was an airplane. "When I heard the slugs tearing into the gas tank, I knew I had to set down quick, but there was nothing clear for miles around."

Cody leaned forward and waited for more.

"So I aimed for a spot where the jungle would break my fall, and I crash landed it as best I could."

Grandpa continued: "I came in hot, and I hit hard. I was bleeding pretty bad and my leg was broken, but I had to get out of there. So I pulled myself out and got as far away as I could. I got away just as the fuel tank blew."

Cody was totally captivated.

"So there I was, well behind enemy lines, in bad shape with no food. Didn't even have the med kit because it was back there, all burned to ashes. But what do you do? You do what you can do. I ripped up my shirt for bandages and then I hacked off some branches with a sharp piece of metal from the wreckage and I made myself a splint for my leg.

"I knew there was a base somewhere to the north. It took me several days of crawling through the jungle, eating beetles and digging up roots."

Cody did some serious thinking that night. He wasn't too proud of himself for all the griping he'd been doing.

Grandpa had nearly died so many times when he was at war. And to hear him tell it, it was always an adventure. Cody had never heard him complain even once.

After school on Monday, Cody hustled to Pioneer Park for some secret practice. He figured if he practiced twice as much, he'd get better twice as fast.

It felt weird to go play by himself, without Mud or any of his teammates. But Cody could barely look at Mud lately. He just felt so ashamed. Cody couldn't believe how mean he had been to Mud when all Mud was doing was trying to be his best. All Cody wanted to do was apologize. But for some reason the words just never came out.

Cody hoped it would be easier to apologize if he was playing better.

So he worked. He ran wind sprints—up the hill, around the hill, up the hill again—until he collapsed and had to lie down while his side unstitched itself.

Then he practiced his ball skills. First he just worked on turns. But then he got really crazy. Before he left for the night, Cody practiced a spin move. As he spun, he moved the ball back with one foot and then pulled it back with his other foot as it turned forward again. As the sun started to go down, Cody could almost do it at full speed—with no defender, of course.

At the Lions' next practice, Cody was sort of hoping that he might have magically gotten better overnight.

⦀⦀

Nope.

Cody tried to pull off his new spin move right away during the scrimmage. But right away, Trong stuck his foot in and tapped the ball away. As Cody lost his balance and fell on his side, he watched as Mud received the ball and ran up the field.

The old Cody probably would have started complaining and given up right there. But he kept thinking of his grandpa crawling on his belly in that swamp, just to stay alive.

So Cody picked himself up and ran back down the field. He kept running hard for the rest of practice. Then he went home and kept working on his spin move. And even though Mrs. Stoutner was loading on the math homework, Cody kept up that routine every day for the next two weeks.

And the Lions actually won their first game, against the Holborn Highlanders. And then they won again. And again. And again! Cody even got the assist in the game-winning goal in the third game. And suddenly the Lions found themselves in the mix for the league championship game.

Cody practiced extra hard the next day. Wind sprints were getting easier, and he spent more time working on his spin move and other dekes. So he didn't notice that it had gotten pretty dark, until he heard crying.

Cody pushed in closer. All he saw was Nik Danker and his friends towering over this kid from Cody's math class, Tommy Lin.

Nik Danker was in seventh grade. And not only was he the biggest kid in their school, he was the biggest kid Cody had ever seen. Word around the school was that he worked out by bench-pressing fifth graders.

Tommy's books were scattered all over the ground. He looked totally terrified.

Maybe Cody was taking Grandpa's talk about heroism to heart. Or maybe he was just mad. He went right up and got in Nik's face. "Cut it out!"

Nik and his cronies stopped cold. Maybe no one had ever done that to him.

Tommy snatched up his books and ran off faster than Cody had ever seen anyone run before.

Now it was just Cody and Nik and his two minions.

Then Cody's brain kicked in. He had just made Nik Danker really mad.

Nik shoved Cody in the chest.

"Think you're so much better than me, huh?"

Cody looked around frantically. Nik's friends laughed like all the super villains Cody had ever seen on TV.

Maybe Cody could try running away. But they were a lot bigger and stronger than him. And he'd just been doing wind sprints all afternoon. His legs felt like jelly and probably had three steps left in them before they'd fold under him and drop him to the ground where he would get kicked to death.

There was no way out.

SEVEN

As he watched them close in, Cody knew he was done for. If he'd been one of those strong strikers like Ryan, he might have stood a chance. But it was just him. Cody Ross, fifth grader. He wished he was playing the *Street Fighter* video game instead of really fighting in the street.

Cody could just see his mom standing over his mangled body, weeping into the TV cameras. "Why did he have to try to be a hero?"

Nik had this really nasty look on his face, and Cody knew he was about to get it. Nik spat a humungous loogie on the ground and smiled this slow nasty smile at Cody. That was when Cody heard a rustling in the woods behind him.

"Hey, cut it out!" the voice said.

Was it . . . Mudman? Cody turned around to see his friend. And with him were Ryan and Trong and Mahender and a bunch of the other guys.

Cody let out a sigh of relief. Briefly.

"Oh yeah," Nik howled. "And what are you going to do about it?"

Then Amanda stepped out from behind Mahender.

"I'm going to tell the principal," she said, as a look of fear took over Nik's face. After all, the principal was Amanda's mom, and if Nik got in trouble one more time he would be kicked off the wrestling team.

Cody felt like smiling, but he did his best to keep it in.

"Psh." Nik tried to play it cool.

"Come on guys," he told his buddies, and they walked away from the park.

Cody sighed, and then he let out a big, relieved smile.

"Thanks, guys!"

"The Mudman told us you might be here," Amanda replied.

"Yeah," Trong added. "He told us you had an awesome spin move that we all had to see. Like, you do a 360 with the ball?"

Startled, Cody's eyes shot toward Mud, who was looking down at his feet. *How did Mud know I'd been practicing?* Cody wondered.

Then he wondered it out loud.

"How'd you know I had been practicing?" Cody demanded.

"Well," Mud said sheepishly, "it was always your favorite move in *Soccer Slam*."

Oh, yeah.

"And Ryan was talking about how he wanted to learn how to do it."

Just then, Cody remembered how well Mud knew him. After all, only Mud would have known that Cody would try to mimic his favorite video game moves. He always shouted out "Whoo!" as he passed a helpless defender in *Soccer Slam*.

But, wait a minute. Ryan? *Ryan* wanted help learning a move?

"But Ryan's got the best footwork on the team," Cody said, almost bewildered.

"Yeah," Amanda stepped forward. "And Trong has the best shot on the team. So we can all work together and give each other tips."

"Mud has been telling us all season how cool of a guy you are," Trong said. "So we figured we should all hang out together."

"And win a championship!" Ryan called out.

Cody shot a glance over to Mud, who now returned the look. Instantly they both smiled. Neither had to say a word. They just knew they were best friends again.

EIGHT

The Lions practiced only two days per week. But the players began hanging out just about every other day.

They went to the park to teach each other tricks. They watched videos of awesome soccer goals online. At school, they even traveled in packs, just in case Nik Danker and his buddies tried to give them trouble.

And on the soccer field, the Lions were starting to get good. Really good.

They beat the Wolverton Wolverines, who actually weren't all that ferocious.

Then they played a tough game with the Manchester Mice, who were a lot tougher than they sounded. The Mice made the Lions fight hard for every goal.

Pretty soon the Lions were on a five-game winning streak. One more win would put them in the championship.

The final game was all the way over in Alton. That meant all the kids had to pile into their parents' cars and drive almost two hours. But it was well worth it.

The Alton Giants were pretty good, but they were no match for the Lions. And despite their team name, the players were hardly giant. Mud made a perfect pass to Ryan for a goal in the first half. Then Trong and Amanda each scored in the second half. After each one, the whole team surrounded the goal scorer and cheered. And Cody had made a pass in the run-up to all three goals.

As Cody and Mud exchanged their secret handshake after the game, Cody couldn't help but notice how much he was smiling. He was really part of the team now.

The win meant the Lions had made the championship game. It would be a rematch against the Watertown Waves. That was the team that had beaten the Lions in the season opener. It was also the team that Cody had scored an own-goal for.

But this time, he was ready to take revenge.

The Lions chose two players to be the team captains each game. In the championship, they picked Cody and Mud.

Mud had been a captain before, but this was Cody's first time. As they walked to the center of the field for the pre-game coin toss, Cody couldn't help but feel proud. So, apparently, did Mud.

"We've been looking really good in practice," he blurted out. "I think this time we might actually win a championship together."

The referee waited at midfield. Then Watertown's captains showed up as well. One of them was the big guy. The mustache was gone—maybe it had been a stain after all. But he was certainly still quite large.

This time, Cody was not afraid. He'd faced down Nik Danker and his goons in the woods. Now he knew that his teammates would be behind him if Mr. Mustache tried anything cheap.

The Waves won the coin toss—Cody knew he should have called "heads!"—and started with the ball.

Neither team held onto it too much after that, though. The game went back and forth, with each team playing stellar defense.

Cody sat down on a cooler and sucked the juice out of an orange slice at halftime. It felt like he had run a marathon already, and yet he'd barely touched the ball. Coach Parks was apparently just as confident as his players had been, though.

"Just keep doing what you're doing," he told them at halftime. "You keep doing that and we'll get our break soon enough."

It didn't come soon enough, though. The game remained scoreless late in the second half.

And all of those wind sprints didn't seem to matter anymore. Cody was winded. He barely had time to rest, though. As soon as he placed his hands on his knees and took a deep breath, he heard his name.

"Cody!" Ryan hollered. "Behind you, he's about to make a run!"

Sure enough, the Waves' fastest player was starting a run up the sideline. If Cody didn't start now, the Waves' player would be wide open. So Cody put his head down and booked after him.

"Look up!" a voice yelled out.

Cody did. He saw a pass rolling toward the Waves player. In an instant—without even thinking about it—Cody dropped to the ground for a slide tackle. His toe was pointed just enough to catch the edge of the ball. It rolled out of bounds as the Waves player tumbled over Cody.

"Nice work, Codes!"

He looked and saw his parents on the sideline cheering for him.

Cody smiled, and then reached out to grab Ryan's arm.

"Great tackle," Ryan said as he pulled Cody up. "I'm glad you didn't go out for striker. That's some nice D."

"That's why I like playing midfield," Cody said back to Ryan with a smile. "I get to play a little bit of offense and defense."

((((((

The Waves threw the ball in, but their players must have been tired too. The guy who had scored three times against the Lions in the first game received the ball, but Mahender came in and easily came away with it.

"Let's go!"

At first Cody was startled. He'd never heard Coach Parks that loud or that intense.

But then he was motivated.

Cody took off down the right sideline, glancing over to see Mahender pass the ball to Amanda, who passed it to Ryan, who then passed it off to Mud.

Then Cody looked up, and his heart started to race even faster.

"I'm open!" he screamed as he ran toward the penalty box.

Before he knew it, a pass from Mud was on its way right into Cody's path.

In a video game this would be a sure goal. The ball would stick to the players' feet, Cody would toggle the joystick to run around the defender, speed burst toward the goal, and unleash a hard shot by holding down the A button.

But this was real life. And as soon as the ball bounced off Cody's right foot, he realized Mr. Mustache was the last man standing between him and the goalie.

Cody didn't need a controller this time. He tapped the ball once with his right foot and twice with his left foot. Mr. Mustache couldn't believe it—was Cody dribbling the ball right at him?

Mr. Mustache got down into a defensive position, but by then it was already too late.

Just like he'd practiced, Cody tapped the ball twice as he spun over it and cruised around the defender.

The crowd gasped. Not even Coach Parks could believe it.

Cody took one more touch on the ball. Then he remembered what Trong had taught him about shooting.

The next thing he remembered was being at the bottom of a hog pile.

"You did it, Cody!"

"What a move!"

"I can't believe it!"

"We are the champions!"

"Yes *we* are!" Cody hollered, knowing that it was Mahender's steal and Amanda's set up and Mud's assist and Trong's advice that had led to his miracle goal. And, of course, there was Cody's spin move. He couldn't help but feel that the hard work had paid off.

((((((

One by one, Cody's teammates eventually climbed off the hog pile. It was like a breath of fresh air when Cody was finally free.

Mud reached out and pulled Cody back to his feet. Giant smiles burst across their faces as they went into their secret handshake.

"Nice work, Codes!"

"Hey, you're the star, Mudman!"

They had barely finished the handshake when they noticed all of their teammates rushing over to a table set up near the midfield line. They looked at the table, then they looked back at each other.

"Trophies!" they called out as they sprinted over to accept their hardware.

Each trophy had a player lining up to take a hard shot—just like the ones Trong took. As Cody admired the shiny statue in front of him, he couldn't help but think it looked a little bit cooler than the tinfoil star he and Mud had made.

As the clicking and flashing died down from the parents' cameras, Cody noticed his parents coming over to him.

"What a game!" his dad said.

"We're really proud of you," his mom added.

Cody's dad patted Cody on the back. Cody couldn't help but feel pretty good.

"I'll tell you what, Codes," his dad said. "I've talked to some of the parents, and I'm going to cook up some juicy bison burgers for a little team banquet at our place."

"And," his mom added, "if you want you guys can play a *Soccer Slam* tournament while we eat." Cody's ears perked up when he heard that.

Then he felt something bump into the side of his leg.

"Sounds great guys," he said as he leaned down and picked up the soccer ball that had rolled into him. "But I think we'd rather play a different game—in the backyard."

THE END